哈福

可以馬上學會的超強生活美語

張瑪麗・Scott William 合著

附 **MP3**

無壓力
輕鬆學習法
★★★

哈福

假如學英語
像看小說一樣輕鬆

假如你讀過作者英語專家張瑪麗的一系列英語教材，你的一口純正美語、遣詞用字必定讓許多人印象深刻了吧！恭喜你的成就！而如果這是你首度閱讀張瑪麗的著作，恭喜你，這將會是改變你一生的機會！把握住，跟著學，一步一步來，你會很訝異自己進步的神速！

現在，告訴我，與學習英語比較起來，你是否覺得讀短篇小說會更悠閒一些？假如學習英語能像看小說一般，你是否會覺得更輕鬆！是的，我們這一套書的目的，就是要讓你在「輕鬆自如」的氣氛中，像讀小說一般，無壓力地學會英語。

本書也將英語最常用的文法、語法、常用語等，以你最能容易明白的說明，詳盡解析，使你在學習時，會有「啊，英語原來是這麼一回事！」的徹悟，從根本建立起自己的英語自信！

2

用最簡單的單字、句子，說出生活中的所有英語，每天念、每天說、每天進步，日積月累，你也可以成為英語高手！

所以，放輕鬆，像看小說一樣，看看我們的英語短篇小說，同時像聽廣播劇一樣地聽本書所附贈的 MP3，熟悉純正美語的發音與說話的語氣，讓你周遭的人、你所接觸的英美人士讚嘆你的英語能力吧！

英語高手的 秘密武器：英文法

學英文法的神話：不需要學英文法？

如果你認為美國小孩子不需要學英文法，那你就大錯特錯了，美國從小學一年級起，到高中三年級的英語的教科書裡，都有教英文法。美國學生同樣要學主詞、動詞、形容詞和動詞時式等等，你我皆耳熟能詳的英文法。

英文法可以把英文的用法、說法做一個歸類，使學習英語更為輕鬆。要成為英語高手，可得把這項秘密武器練好哦。

如何成為英語高手

誰是英語高手？英語高手是怎麼個高法？當然是那些遇到老美可以輕鬆自如的跟老美聊天的人囉，換句話說，重點就是在「輕鬆自如」這四個字上面。

當你跟老美聊天時，不要腦子裡一個勁兒地想著中文，然後，絞盡腦汁來把這些中文翻譯成英文，想想看你那種場面，怎麼輕鬆的起來呢？而且講出來的英語，肯定是洋涇濱英語。

怎麼能算是英語高手呢，所以，你要知道，人家跟你說甚麼話，你要用哪句話回答。如何做到呢，就是要記住一些最基本的句型。為什麼要記基本句型，它的功用就是我們的英語高手一直在強調的，這樣才能輕鬆自如的跟老美聊天，而不會苦著臉在想著這句中文如何翻譯成英語，而是能夠流利的脫口說出你要說的話。

說英語就是這麼簡單

你有沒有注意到，我們的英語高手一直在教你一個很簡單的英語學習法，這個方法就是人類學習語言不變的原則，也就是我們一直強調的「自然英語學習法」。人類如何學習語言呢，想想

看小孩子怎麼學語言吧，那就是大人說一句，他們就跟著牙牙的學，到有一天，他們的腦子裡就會整理出一套規則，知道什麼時候用哪一句話來說，所以，我們的英語高手，也是一直在告訴你，老美什麼時候，說甚麼話，你只要跟著我們的英語高手學，很快的，你也會成為一位英語高手，很簡單的。

美國人怎麼說，我們也跟著說

如何說一口流利的英語呢？很簡單，就是，美國人怎麼說，我們就跟著那麼說，就對了，這種英語學習法，就是我們一貫強調的「自然英語學習法」，學習英語絕不應該是「逐字翻譯」，也不用把「說英語」當成一門高深的學問，挑燈苦讀，說英語，應該是跟你說中文一樣，自自然然地，美國人怎麼說，我們就跟著這麼說，當然，我們學英語的環境跟學中文的環境不一樣。

所以如何跟著美國人自自然然地說英語，就是美國 AA Bridgers 公司，一直在為大家做的工作，我們提供給大家美國人每天說的英語，讓各位跟著說，你只要每天跟著說，自然會說一口流利的英語。

目錄

Life English

English

MEMO

FAST & EASY

假如學英語像看小說

Smith家小孩放學回家

黃昏時候，Lisa正在廚房裡，忙著為將下班和放學回來的丈夫、小孩準備晚餐，Lisa有一個正在念高中的女兒，還有兩個活潑可愛的小孩，Billy八歲，Jenny七歲。 Lisa一邊做飯，一邊想著兩個小孩應該很快到家了，果然，她聽到兩個小孩進門來了，Lisa就開口問他們，今天在學校裡還好嗎？

Hey guys, how was school?

（嗨，你們兩個小傢伙，今天在學校還好吧？）

Jenny是個聰明、伶俐，有點頑皮愛說話)小女孩，聽到媽媽問他們，她就迫不及待地搶著回答，

I had fun today.

（我在學校很愉快。）

We got to color and we had a snack.

（我們有畫圖著色，還吃點心。）

Lisa聽到就回答她說，

That's great.

（那很棒。）

I'm glad you had fun.

（我很高興你在學校裡很愉快。）

而且Lisa知道，Billy比較沈靜，不會像他妹妹一樣搶著說話，所以，Lisa就問Billy說，

How about you, Billy?

（比利，你呢？）

How did it go?

（你在學校怎麼樣？）

Billy雖然比較安靜，但是他是一個很聰明的小孩子，他很喜歡學習新的事物，今天在學校裡，科學課教了一些他很有興趣的東西，所以他就興高采烈地告訴Lisa說，

We are learning something new in science.

（我們的科學課在學一些新的東西。）

Lisa表示興趣的繼續問道，

Really?

（真的！？）

Tell me about it.

（說來聽聽。）

Really?
Tell me about it.

Billy就告訴他媽媽，他們現在在學植物，所以，在學校裡，老師帶他們去採樹葉回來研究，

We are learning about plants.

（我們在學植物。）

So, we went on a nature walk and picked up leaves.

（所以，我們到野外去，摘了一些樹葉。）

12

Lisa知道這是她兒子最有興趣的事，所以她也以很興奮的口吻跟他說，

Wow!

（哇！）

That sounds like a lot of fun.

（聽起來蠻有趣的。）

Billy雖然覺得在學校所做的是很有趣，但是放學回到家，他覺得很累了，所以，跟他媽媽說，

It was but now I'm tired.

（是很有趣，但是，我累了。）

Lisa跟Billy說的很高興，Jenny在一旁不甘被冷落，聽到Billy說他累了，她也趕緊插嘴說，她也累了，

Me too!

（我也是。）

Billy又繼續說，

And I'm starving.

（我肚子很餓。）

Jenny也頗有同感的說，

Me too!

（我也是。）

Billy想吃東西,所以問媽媽說,

Is there anything to eat?

(有沒有什麼東西可以吃?)

Lisa在白天裡,做了一些小餅乾,所以她說,

Well, I did make some cookies.

(嗯,我是做了一些小餅乾。)

You can have a few before you start your homework.

（你去做功課之前，可以吃一點。）

But don't eat too many.

（但是，不要吃太多。）

I don't want you to spoil your dinner.

（否則，晚飯會吃不下。）

Jenny一聽有小餅乾，趕緊問道，

Can I have some cookies, too?

（我也可以吃一點嗎？）

Lisa哪有只讓Billy吃餅乾，不給Jenny吃的道理，Jenny問她可以吃嗎，Lisa當然說，行，你可以吃，

Of course you can.

（你當然可以吃。）

英語高手的秘密武器：英文法

動詞時式：

1. 過去式
2. 現在進行式

助動詞：

1. Can「請求對方的許可」
2. Can「表示允許」

1. 動詞時式

過去式

　　過去式，顧名思義就是說「過去發生的事情」，聽起來很簡單，但是中國人在說英語時，每每說到過去發生的事情，都還是用現在簡單式在說，以致於老美搞不清楚，根本不知道你是在講一件過去發生的事。

　　說英語時，如果這件過去發生的事情有提到時間，例如：昨天、去年、上星期等等，那麼，一般人大半會知道要用過去式，問題是，有很多情形，說話的當兒根本不提時

間，但是卻是在說一件過去的事，這種情形，中國人說英語時，常常忘了用過去式來說，例如：你回到家，跟你家人說，「在學校我們玩得很愉快」，你說的當然是「一件過去的事情了」。注意這句話一定要用「過去式」。

◆ We had a snack.

（我們有吃點心。）

◆ We had fun at school.

（我們在學校玩得很愉快。）

◆ I got up at 6:00 this morning.

（今天早上我六點起床。）

◆ I made some cookies.

（我做了一些小餅乾。）

注意以下的例句，例如：小孩放學回家來，你問你家小孩，「在學校還好嗎？」，你問的當然是「過去的事情了」，注意這句話一定要用「過去式」，以下的例句，用的都是「be 動詞的過去式 was」。

◆ How was school?

（在學校還好嗎？）

◆ How was your day?

（你今天一整天好嗎？）

◆ How was his meeting?

（他的會議開得如何？）

◆ How was the movie?

（電影好不好看？）

現在進行式

　　現在進行式可以用來表達很多不同的意思，這裡要教的是「現在進行式表示在某一段時間裡，我們在做某件事情」，這裡的某一段時間，指的可能是某一天，或是某幾天，或是一個星期，甚至於，是一個學期或一年，在這段時間裡，我們正在從事於某件事的進行，例如：我最近在看一本很有趣的小說，看小說，不是每天二十四小時都在看，所以我說這話的當兒，我可能正在跟你聊天，所以當我告訴你，我正在看一本有趣的小說，但是，實際上，此時此刻我是在跟你聊天，並沒有在看小說，雖然此時此刻我並沒有在看小說，但是我最近是在看這本小說，而且還沒有看完，我這幾天還會繼續看，這種情形就是我們這裡教的要用「現在進行式」的情形。

現在進行式的說法就是「主詞＋ are，am 或 is ＋現在分詞」，什麼是現在分詞呢，凡是有動作的字，都是一個動詞，例如：吃飯、走路、睡覺、唸書。動詞在某些情況下要改成「現在分詞」，也就是在這個動詞的字尾加 ing。現在進行式，就是其中的一個情況之一。

◆ We are learning about plants.
（我們在學植物。）

◆ I am reading an interesting book.
（我在看一本有趣的書。）

◆ Mary is studying English in America.
（瑪麗在美國讀英語。）

◆ We are building a swimming pool.
（我們在蓋游泳池。）

助動詞

Can可以用來表示「請求對方的許可」

◆ Can I have some cookies, too?
（我也可以吃一些餅乾嗎？）

◆ Can John spend the night?
（約翰可以在這裡過夜嗎？）

◆ Can she come with me?

（她可以跟我一起來嗎？）

◆ Can you help him?

（你可以幫他的忙？）

**Can這個助動詞，可以用來表示
「允許他人做某件事情」**

◆ You can have a few.

（可以給你一些。）

◆ She can come, too.

（她也可以來。）

◆ You can do your homework later.

（你可以稍後再做你的功課。）

◆ John can take this home.

（約翰可以把這個拿回家。）

命令句

命令句的肯定句

◆ Tell me about it.

（說來聽聽看。）

◆ Change your clothes.

（去換衣服。）

◆ Wash your hands.

（去洗手。）

◆ Do your homework.

（去做家庭作業。）

命令句的否定句

◆ Don't eat too many.

（別吃太多。）

◆ Don't spoil your dinner.

（別讓晚餐吃不下。）

◆ Don't stand there.

（別站在那裡。）

◆ Don't run.

（不要跑。）

英語高手的秘密武器：英文法　　21

如何成為英語高手

記住這些基本句型，輕輕鬆鬆跟老美聊天

Is there ~ to
I did ~
We got to ~

Is there ~ to＋原型動詞，這個句型的意思是「有沒有什麼東西，可以…」。

◆ Is there anything to eat?
　　　　（有沒有什麼東西可以吃？）

◆ Is there anything to do?
　　　　（有沒有什麼事可以做？）

◆ Is there anything to drink?
　　　　（有沒有什麼東西可以喝？）

◆ Is there anything to read?
　　　　（有沒有什麼東西可以讀？）

I did＋原型動詞，這句話的意思就是「我的確有做了這件事」。

◆ I did make some cookies.

（我是烤了些小餅乾。）

◆ I did go to the store.

（我是有去店裡買東西。）

◆ I did fill the pitcher.

（我是把罐子裝滿了。）

◆ I did clean the floor.

（我是把地板抹乾淨了。）

We got to +原型動詞，這句話的意思就是「我們有機會做某件事」。

◆ We got to color.

（我們有畫圖。）

◆ We got to tell stories.

（我們有講故事。）

◆ We got to go outside.

（我們有到外面去玩。）

◆ We got to be in the parade.

（我們有參加遊行。）

說英語就是這麼簡單

我也是

I'm starving!

Me too.

當有人說一件事，而你也有同感，要表示
「我也是」，它的英語就是，Me too.

・・・・・・・・・・・・・・・・・

1. A: What's wrong?

（怎麼啦？）

B: I'm starving!

（我餓死了。）

I haven't eaten all day.

（我一整天都沒吃東西。）

24

2. A: I'm starving!

（我餓死了。）

B: Me too.

（我也是。）

Why don't we go have dinner?

（我們何不吃去晚餐？）

A: Okay, let me get my coat.

（好的，我去拿外套。）

3. A: I want to go to the concert this weekend.

（我這個週末要去聽音樂會。）

B: Me too!

（我也是。）

4. A: I've always wanted to go to Egypt.

（我一直都想去埃及玩。）

B: Me too.

（我也是。）

Maybe one day we'll get to.

（或許有一天我們會去得成。）

真的？

Really? That's great.

I made an A on my test!

當有人告訴你一件事情，你要表示對這件事的興趣，有時你會問說，「真的嗎？」，那就說，Really? 就對了。

● ● ● ● ● ● ● ● ● ● ● ● ● ● ● ●

1. A: I made an A on my test!

（我考試拿了 A。）

B: Really? That's great.

（真的？那真好。）

26

2. A: I heard that The Phantom of the Opera is coming to town.

（我聽說「劇院魅影」要來演。）

B: Really?

（真的。）

That's one of my favorite musicals!

（那是我最喜歡的音樂劇之一。）

哇！

Look at that diamond.

Wow! It's huge.

遇到令你覺得很驚喜的事物嗎？Wow!
這個字可以適切地表達你的意思。

1. A: Look at that diamond.
（看看那個鑽石。）

B: Wow!
（哇！）

It's huge.
（好大的鑽石。）

2. A: Check this out.
（你看看。）

B: Wow!
（哇！）

I've never seen so many colors.
（我從沒看過這麼多顏色。）

成為英語高手的基礎：單字、片語

fun [fʌn]	好玩；樂趣
color [`kʌlɚ]	動 著色
snack [snæk]	點心
science [`saɪəns]	科學
plant [plænt]	名 植物
nature [`netʃɚ]	名 天然；自然界
tired [taɪrd]	疲倦的
starve [stɑrv]	動 飢餓
cookies [ˈkʊkiz]	小餅乾
spoil [spɔɪl]	破壞
interesting [`ɪntərɪstɪŋ]	有趣的
build [bɪld]	建造

pool [pul]	名 游泳池
spend [spɛnd]	動 花（時間）
change [tʃendʒ]	動 改變；變更
store [stor]	名 商店
clean [klin]	清理
floor [flor]	地板
fill [fɪl]	裝滿
pitcher [`pɪtʃɚ]	（裝飲料的）大罐子
parade [pə`red]	遊行
concert [`kɑnsɚt]	名 演奏會；音樂會
favorite [`fevərɪt]	最喜歡的
musical [`mjuzɪk!]	名 音樂劇
diamond [`daɪəmənd]	鑽石
huge [hjudʒ]	巨大的

Richard回家吃午飯

Lisa是個家庭主婦,她的先生Richard中午都會回家午飯,休息一下,再回去上班,今天,Richard.吃完午飯還沒休息,就匆匆地要再趕回公司,Lisa正在廚房裡忙著,Richard告訴Lisa,他要回公司了,

Lisa, I'm leaving.

（莉沙,我要走了。）

Lisa在廚房裡聽見了,奇怪她先生怎麼這麼快就要走了,就趕緊出來問Richard說,

Is your lunchtime over already?

（你的午餐時間過了嗎?）

Richard說他的午休時間還沒過,只是他心裡頭惦記著下午要開的一個重要會議,所以要趕緊回公司準備一下,

Not yet but I want to get back early.

（還沒有，但是我想要早一點回公司。）

I have an important meeting and I want some time to prepare for it.

（我有一個很重要的會議，我需要一些時間準備。）

Lisa想起來，這幾天Richard一直在跟她提今天下午這個重要的會議，只是她忘了，

That's right!

（是啊。）

I forgot all about your meeting today.

（我完全忘了你今天的會議。）

Richard當然知道他這位樂天的太太，怎麼會記得這些惱人的事情呢，只是他太太可以不記得，他可是天天擔著心哪！所以他跟他太太說，

I wish I could have.

（我希望我也能把它忘的一乾二淨。）

I'm really worried.

（我真的很擔心。）

This is one of our most important clients.

（這是我們最重要的客戶之一。）

Lisa鼓勵他先生說，別擔心，我知道你可以做得很好。

Don't worry, Richard, I'm sure you'll do fine.

（別擔心，理查，我知道你可以做得很好。）

Richard謝過他太太的鼓勵，並問她下午要做什麼事，

Thanks, honey.

（謝謝你，親愛的。）

What are you going to do this afternoon?

（你今天下午要做什麼？）

Lisa說，她下午會去逛街購物，問Richard需要什麼東西，

I'm going grocery shopping.

（我要去買些東西。）

Do you need anything?

（你需要什麼東西嗎？）

Richard說他不需要什麼東西，但是想請Lisa幫他買一些李子回來，

> *Not really, but I would like some plums.*
>
> （不需要什麼，但是我想要一些李子。）

Lisa回答說，沒問題，

> *Okay then.*
>
> （好的。）

> *I'll try to remember to pick some up.*
>
> （我會盡量記得買一些回來。）

Look. I've got to go.

Richard謝謝他太太，就準備要趕緊回公司了，

Thanks.

（謝謝。）

Well, look. I've got to go.

（那，我該走了。）

Tell the kids I love them and I'll be home soon.

（跟孩子們說，我愛他們，我很快就回來。）

Lisa也催他快走，並祝他會議進行的順利，

I'll do that.

（我會的。）

Now, get out of here.

（快走吧。）

Good luck at your meeting and I'll see you tonight.

（祝你的會議順利，今天晚上見。）

英語高手的秘密武器：英文法

動詞時式：

1. 未來式
2. 現在進行式
3. 命令句的肯定
4. 命令句的否定

1. 動詞時式

未來式

當你要說，「我會這麼做時」，你是在說一件，在「未來的時間」你要做的事情，這種情形，就是英文法裡說的「未來式」，「未來式」的用法就是「will ＋原型動詞」。

◆ I'll be home soon.

（我很快回來。）

◆ I'll see you tonight.

（今晚再見。）

◆ I'll try to remember.

（我會盡量記得。）

◆ I'll do that.

（我會去做。）

現在進行式

當你要表示「我現在正要去做這件事」時，要用「現在進行式」，表示你即將去做，「現在進行式」的用法是「be＋現在分詞」。

◆ I'm leaving.
◆ I'm going.
◆ I'm moving.

用 **be going to** ＋原型動詞，表示「已經計畫好要做的動作」。

當某件事情已經決定要做了，這件將要做的事情，當然要用「未來式」了，要說某人已經決定好要做某件事情，英語的說法就是「某人 is going to ＋原型動詞」這種英語說法，就是用在當你想說，「某人打算要…」，「某人將會…」，「某人要…」，或是「某人會…」時。如果我們確知某件事將會如何時，它的說法就是「某件事 is going to be ＋形容詞」。

這種英語說法，就是用在當你想說，「某件事將會…」時。

◆ What are you going to do?

（你打算要做什麼？）

◆ What are you going to wear?

（你打算要穿什麼衣服？）

◆ What are you going to tell him?

（你打算要告訴他什麼？）

◆ What are you going to cook for dinner?

（你晚餐要煮什麼？）

命令句

命令句的肯定句

◆ Tell the kids I love them.

（告訴孩子們，我愛他們。）

◆ Get out of here.

（快走吧。）

◆ Call me tonight.

（今晚打電話給我。）

◆ Turn off the TV.

（把電視機關掉。）

命令句的否定

◆ Don't worry.

（別擔心。）

◆ Don't forget.

（別忘記。）

◆ Don't talk.

（別說話。）

◆ Don't cry.

（別哭。）

如何成為英語高手

記住這些基本句型，輕輕鬆鬆跟老美聊天

1. I'm really + 形容詞！
2. Is 某件東西 already ~

I'm really＋形容詞，這句話表示「我真的很…」。

◆ I'm really worried.

（我真的很擔心。）

◆ I'm really hungry.

（我真的很餓。）

◆ I'm really tired.

（我真的很累。）

◆ I'm really excited.

（我真的很興奮。）

Is某件東西already ~ ， 這句話表示「某件事情已經…了嗎？」，Is某人already ~ ，這句話表示「某人已經…了嗎？」。

◆ Is your lunchtime over already?

（你的午餐時間已經過了嗎？）

◆ Is the movie already over?

（電影已經演完了嗎？）

◆ Is your homework already finished?

（你的功課已經做完了嗎？）

◆ Is John here already?

（約翰已經來了嗎？）

說英語就是這麼簡單

我來做，我會去做。

I'll do that.

當有人要求你做某件事情，而你也答應會去做，你的回答就是，I'll do that.

. . . .

1. A: Be sure to finish your homework.
（一定要做完你的功課哦。）

B: I will.
（我會的。）

A: And take out the trash too, please.
（還要把垃圾拿出去丟。）

B: Okay, I'll do that.

（好的，我會去做。）

2. A: Could someone answer the phone?

（誰有空去接個電話？）

B: I'll do that.

（我來接。）

Good luck.

> Good luck on your exam.

> Thanks, good luck to you too.

當你知道某人要做一件事情，這件事情能不能做的成，還說不定時，你就可以跟他說聲，Good luck. 這句話表達了，你希望他要去做的這件事做的成，或做的好的意思。

1. A: I've got to get this project finished by Friday.
   （星期五之前，我一定得把企畫作完）

   B: Good luck!
   （希望你做的完）

2. A: Good luck on your exam.
   （祝你考的好。）

   B: Thanks, good luck to you, too.
   （謝謝，也祝你考的好。）

44

成為英語高手的基礎：單字、片語

early [`ɚlɪ]	早
important [ɪm`pɔrtn̩t]	形 重要的
meeting [`mitɪŋ]	會議
prepare [prɪ`pɛr]	準備
forgot [fɚ`gɑt]	忘記（forget 的過去式）
worried [`wɝɪd]	憂心的；擔心的（過去分詞當形容詞用。）
really [`rɪəlɪ]	真的
client [`klaɪənt]	客戶
grocery [`grosərɪ]	雜貨
plum [plʌm]	李子
remember [rɪ`mɛmbɚ]	記得
luck [lʌk]	運氣

wear [wɛr]	動 穿
cook [kʊk]	動 烹調；煮
kid [kɪd]	小孩子
worry [`wɝɪ]	動 憂慮；擔心
forget [fɚ`gɛt]	忘記
cry [kraɪ]	哭
hungry [`hʌŋgrɪ]	餓
excited [ɪk`saɪtɪd]	感到興奮的
already [ɔl`rɛdɪ]	副 已經
finished [`fɪnɪʃt]	完成了（finish 的過去分詞）
finish [`fɪnɪʃ]	動 完成
trash [træʃ]	垃圾
project [`prɑdʒɛkt]	專案；企畫
exam [ɪg`zæm]	考試（examination 的縮寫）

一早起來,邁可和母親談話

早上,Michael正要去上學,他的母親Karen也準備好要去上班。Karen一早起來,看見她兒子就跟他說早安,

Good morning, Michael.

（麥可,早。）

Michael也跟他母親說聲,早。

Good morning, Mom.

（媽,您早。）

因為Michael除了上學外,還有兼差上班,貼補家用,所以Karen很關心Michael晚上有沒有睡好,

Did you sleep well?

（你昨晚睡得好嗎?）

Michael因為學校裡有報告要交，所以兼差上班之餘，必須熬夜才能跟得上學校的功課，前一天晚上，Michael為了趕報告，又熬夜了，所以一聽到母親問他有沒有睡好，他回答說，

Not really.
（不太好。）

I was up most of the night doing my report.
（我幾乎整晚熬夜在趕學校的報告。）

Karen更關心他報告有沒有做完，

Did you get it done?
（有沒有做完？）

Michael說，

Yeah, I finally finished it.
（有，總算做完了。）

Karen知道Michael既要上學，又要兼差上班的辛苦，所以體諒的說道，

I know it's hard working and going to school but hang in there.

（我知道，要上班又要上學是很辛苦的，但是，你要忍著點。）

I'm really proud of you.

（我很替你感到驕傲。）

And I know you'll do fine.

（我知道，你可以做得很好。）

Michael很感謝媽媽的體諒和鼓勵，

Thanks, mom.

（謝謝你，媽。）

Michael因為是兼差，所以上班的時間並不是很固定，所以，Karen想知道Michael當晚要不要去工作，

So, do you have work again today?

（那，你今天還要去工作嗎？）

Michael告訴母親，他當晚要去工作，並詳細的跟他母親說，他下班後還要去圖書館，

Yes, and it's going to be very busy.

（是的，今天將會很忙。）

We're having a sale but we're going to close early.

（我們正在拍賣，但是我們今天會早一點打烊。）

So, I should get off around 7:00 tonight.

（所以，我應該七點左右就會下班。）

But I've got to go to the library.

（但是，我必須到圖書館去。）

So, I won't actually get home until after 9:00.

（所以，我九點以後才會回到家。）

Karen也讓Michael知道她也是會晚一點才回來，並要Michael自己叫匹薩餅吃，

Well, I have to work late again, anyway.

（嗯，我反正也會工作到很晚。）

But I should be home by then.

（但是，我那個時候應該會回來。）

50

Do you want to order a pizza for dinner?

（你要叫匹薩餅當晚餐嗎？）

Michael說好，

That sounds good.

（好。）

Karen就跟Michael說再見了，

Okay, I'll see you tonight.

（好，今晚見。）

You have a good day.

（祝你今天一整天都愉快。）

Michael也跟他母親說再見，

You too, Mom.

（我也祝你今天一整天都愉快。）

I'll see you later.

（再見。）

假如學英語像看小說　　*51*

英語高手的秘密武器：英文法

動詞時式

1. 未來式
2. 助動詞
3. 現在簡單式的疑問句
4. 過去簡單式的疑問句

1. 動詞時式

未來式

用 be going to ＋原型動詞，表示「已經計畫好要做的動作」。

當某件事情已經決定要做了，這件將要做的事情，當然要用「未來式」了，要說某人已經決定好要做某件事情，英語的說法就是「某人 is going to ＋原型動詞」這種英語說法，就是用在當你想說，「某人將會…」，「某人要…」，或是「某人會…」時。

　　如果我們確知某件事將會如何時，它的說法就是「某件事 is going to be ＋形容詞」。這種英語說法，就是用在當你想說，「某件事將會…」時。

◆ It's going to be very busy.
（今天將會非常忙碌。）

◆ She's going to join the club.
（她要加入俱樂部。）

◆ He's going to call you later.
（他稍後會打電話給你。）

◆ Mary is going to make supper for us.
（瑪麗會為我們做晚飯。）

助動詞

助動詞did放在主詞的前面，用在「過去式的疑問句」。

◆ Did you sleep well?
（你睡得好嗎？）

◆ Did Mary drive home?
（瑪麗開車回家嗎？）

◆ Did John finish his homework?
（約翰的家庭作業有做完嗎？）

◆ Did he eat all his supper?
（他的晚餐有吃完嗎？）

助動詞**do**放在主詞前面，用在「現在簡單式的疑問句。」

◆ Do you have to work?

（你必須工作嗎？）

◆ Do you want to order a pizza?

（你想要叫匹薩餅來吃嗎？）

◆ Do you take a bus to work?

（你都是搭公車上班嗎？）

◆ Do you feel like going out?

（你想出去走走嗎？）

54

如何成為英語高手

記住這些基本句型，輕輕鬆鬆跟老美聊天

動詞時式

finally
I'll see you.

---

finally這個字，用來表示「某人終於…了。」

◆ I finally finished it.
（我終於做完了。）

◆ He finally got a job.
（他終於找到工作了。）

◆ They finally called me.
（他們終於打電話給我了。）

◆She finally graduated.

（她終於畢業了。）

I'll see you.這句話，是用在「道別」的時候。

◆I'll see you tonight.

（今晚見。）

◆I'll see you later.

（再見。）

◆I'll see you after a while.

（以後再見。）

◆I'll see you in the morning.

（明天早上見。）

說英語就是這麼簡單

Not really

Are you ready for your exam?

Not really.

當有人問你一件事，你要說「沒有」的時候，你可以不用直接了當的說 no，可以說 Not really. 表示「沒有」或「不」的意思。

. . . .

1. A: Are you ready for your exam?
   （你考試準備好了嗎？）

   B: Not really.
   （還沒。）

   I need to study a lot more.
   （我還需要再多讀一些。）

2. A: Do you like the cake?
（你喜歡這個蛋糕嗎？）

B: Not really.
（不太喜歡。）

It is a bit too sweet.
（有一點太甜。）

Sounds good.

Sounds good.

Do you want to g
to the movies?

當有人提議去做某件事，而你也覺得這個意見很好，
你同意這麼做，你就可以回答，Sounds good.

1. A: Do you want to go to the movies?
（你要不要一起去看電影？）

B: Sounds good.
（好啊。）

2. A: I'm so hungry for pizza.
（我好餓，想吃披薩餅。）

B: That sounds good.
（好。）

We should order one.
（我們應該叫一個披薩餅。）

英語高手的秘密武器：英文法　　**59**

You too.

Have a good weekend.

You too.

在分手的時候，除了說「再見」以外，你也可以說，「祝你愉快」，當有人跟你說「祝你愉快」時，你回答對方說，You too. 就沒錯了。You too. 的意思就是說「我也同樣祝你愉快」。

1. A: Have a good weekend.

（祝你週末愉快。）

B: You too.

（也祝你週末愉快。）

2. A: Have a nice day.

（祝你一天都很愉快。）

B: You too.

（我也祝你一天都很愉快。）

成為英語高手的基礎：單字、片語

report [rɪ`port]		報告
finally [`faɪnḷɪ]		最終；終於
hard [hɑrd]		困難的
proud [praʊd]		感到驕傲
busy [`bɪzɪ]		忙的
sale [sel]		拍賣
actually [`æktʃʊəlɪ]	副	實際上；事實上
anyway [`ɛnɪˌwe]		無論如何；反正
order [`ɔrdɚ]	動	點菜
later [`letɚ]		稍後
join [dʒɔɪn]		加入
club [klʌb]		俱樂部；社團

supper [ˈsʌpɚ]	晚餐
drive [draɪv]	動 開車
graduate [ˈgrædʒʊˌet]	畢業
ready [ˈrɛdɪ]	準備好
sweet [swit]	甜的
sound [saʊnd]	動 聽起來
weekend [ˈwikˈɛnd]	名 週末

Richard下班回家

Richard是個標準的上班族,每天上班下班,他的太太Lisa是個標準的家庭主婦,每天Richard下班回來,Lisa都在家裡等著,當天Richard工作到很晚才回來,Lisa問他,今天在公司好嗎?

Hey, sweetie, how was your day?

（嗨,親愛的,今天還好嗎?）

Richard覺得一整天上班很累,所以覺得好像過了很長的一天,所以他回答說,

Long. Very long.

（真是忙壞了。）

假如學英語像看小說　**63**

Richard也反問他太太，一整天過的好嗎？

How about yours?

（你呢，今天怎麼樣？）

Lisa回答說，還好，

It was okay.

（還好。）

I did some shopping and I talked to Karen.

（我去買了些東西，還跟凱倫談了一下子。）

We are going to have lunch together on Saturday.

（我們星期六要一起去吃午飯。）

Richard說，很好，

That's great.

I'm glad she called.

（我很高興她打電話來。）

Lisa知道Richard那天有一個很重要的會議，所以她很關心會議開得怎麼樣，

Tell me about your day.

（告訴我你今天在公司裡的情形。）

Nothing bad happened at the meeting, did it?
（會議上，沒出什麼差錯吧？）

Richard告訴Lisa會議沒
有出什麼差錯，但是一切都
還沒有談妥，

No, nothing bad.

（沒有，沒出什麼差錯。）

It's just that our client won't commit.
（只是，客戶還不肯簽約。）

He keeps changing his demands.
（他一直在改變他的要求。）

We can't seem to satisfy him.
（我們好像沒辦法令他滿意。）

Lisa只好要Richard放寬心，別太擔憂，並且安慰他說，有些人
就是那個樣子。

Well, try not to worry about it too much.
（嗯，別太擔心。）

Some people are just like that.
（有些人就是那個樣子。）

I'm sure things will get better soon.
（我相信事情應該很快就會有好結果。）

Richard當然希望事情就像他太太所說的，

I hope you're right.
（我希望你是對的。）

I'd like to finish up this account by the end of the week.
（我想要在這個週末把這個客戶搞定。）

談完工作，Richard話鋒一轉，問起孩子們，

So, are the kids in bed?
（那，孩子們去睡覺了嗎？）

Lisa告訴Richard，孩子們都上床了，不過她知道孩子們應該還沒睡，

Yes, they've already gone to bed.
（是的，他們已經上床了。）

But I doubt they're asleep.
（但是，我想他們應該還沒睡。）

Richard就決定去看看孩子們睡了沒，

Good, I'm going to go peek in on them.
（好，我去偷偷瞧他們一下。）

Maybe I'll tell them a story if they're still awake.
（如果他們還沒睡，或許我會講個故事給他們聽。）

Lisa認為那很好，

I think they'd like that a lot.
（我想，他們會很喜歡聽你講故事。）

Richard告訴他太太Lisa，他看看孩子，很快就會下樓來，

Okay, I'll be back downstairs in a minute.
（好，我很快就下樓來。）

Lisa叫Richard別急，她會趁Richard去看孩子的時間，把晚餐熱一熱，

Take your time.
（別急。）

While you visit with them, I'll heat your dinner up.
（你去看他們的時間，我會把你的晚餐熱一熱。）

英語高手的秘密武器：英文法

1. 動詞時式
1. 未來式
2. 助動詞
   can't 表示「做不到，能力有所不殆」
3. 附加問句

未來式

用 be going to ＋原型動詞，表示「已經計畫好要做的動作」。

當某件事情已經決定要做了，這件將要做的事情，當然要用「未來式」了，要說某人已經決定好要做某件事情，英語的說法就是「某人 is going to ＋原型動詞」這種英語說法，就是用在當你想說，「某人將會…」，「某人要…」，或是「某人會…」時。

如果我們確知某件事將會如何時，它的說法就是「某件事 is going to be ＋形容詞」。這種英語說法，就是用在當你想說，「某件事將會…」時。

◆ We are going to have lunch together.
（我們要一起去吃午餐。）

◆ They are going to visit their grandparents.
（他們要去看他們的祖父母。）

◆ He is going to the dentist on Tuesday.
（他星期二要去看牙醫師。）

◆ We are going to have a party this Friday.
（我們星期五將辦個宴會。）

助動詞

用**can't**這個助動詞，表示「做不到，能力有所不殆」．

◆ We can't seem to satisfy him.
（我們似乎沒辦法令他滿意。）

◆ I can't make the car start.
（我沒辦法開動這部車子。）

◆ She can't open the door.
（她沒辦法把門打開。）

◆ He can't come this evening.
（他今晚沒辦法來。）

英語高手的秘密武器：英文法 **69**

附加問句

Did it

◆ Nothing bad happened at the meeting, did it?
（會議上，沒出什麼差錯吧？）

◆ That didn't hurt, did it?
（那不會痛吧？）

◆ The dog didn't tear that up, did it?
（那隻狗沒有把那件東西撕破吧？）

◆ It didn't break, did it?
（它沒有破吧？）

如何成為英語高手

記住這些基本句型，輕輕鬆鬆跟老美聊天

- Maybe ~
- While you ~ I'll ~.

Maybe這個字，用來表示「或許某人會這麼做」。

◆ Maybe I'll tell them a story.
　　　　（或許我會講個故事給他們聽。）

◆ Maybe I'll call you later.
　　　　（或許我稍後會打電話給你。）

◆ Maybe she can come with us.
　　　　（或許她可以跟我們一起來。）

◆ Maybe we should go now.
　　　　（或許我們現在應該走。）

> **While you ~ , I'll ~.**這個句型，用來表示「當對方在做某件事的時候，你要去做另外一件事。」

◆ While you eat, I'll wash the dishes.
（你在吃飯的時候，我要去洗碗。）

◆ While you watch TV, I'll do my homework.
（你在看電視的時候，我要去做我的功課。）

◆ While you read the paper, I'll take a bath.
（你在看報紙的時候，我要去洗澡。）

◆ While you change clothes, I'll get the car.
（你在換衣服的時候，我去開車。）

說英語就是這麼簡單

Some people are just like that.

Some people are just like that.

My teacher is always mad.

當有人跟你抱怨另外一個人時，你可以安慰他說，Some people are just like that.（有人就是那個樣子。），表示你的精神支持。

1. A: My teacher is always mad.
（我的老師總是在生氣。）

B: Don't worry about it.
（別擔心。）

Some people are just like that.
（有人就是那個樣子。）

2. A: Why does he always make fun of everything?
（他為什麼總是嘲笑每一件事情？）

B: Some people are just like that.
（有些人就是那樣。）

Peek in on.

英語 Peek in on 就是偷偷瞧一瞧的意
思，假如要提議偷偷去看別人在做什麼，
英語就是 Peek in on them and see.

74

1. A: What are the kids doing?

（孩子們在做什麼？）

B: I don't know.

（我不知道。）

Peek in on them and see.

（你去偷瞄一下，看看他們在什麼。）

2. A: How do you know what we're having for dinner?

（你怎麼知道，我們晚餐要吃什麼？）

B: I just peeked in on mom and saw her making it.

（我剛剛去偷瞄了一下媽，看到她在煮什麼。）

成為英語高手的基礎：單字、片語

shopping [`ʃɑpɪŋ]	購物
glad [glæd]	高興
happen [`hæpən]	發生
commit [kə`mɪt]	動 承諾
demand [dɪ`mænd]	名 要求
seem [sim]	似乎
satisfy [`sætɪsˏfaɪ]	動 滿意
soon [sun]	很快地
account [ə`kaʊnt]	名 客戶
doubt [daʊt]	動 懷疑
asleep [ə`slip]	形 睡著的
peek [pik]	偷瞧

awake [ə`wek]	醒著
downstairs [ˌdaʊn`stɛrz]	副 樓下
heat [hit]	動 加熱
dentist [`dɛntɪst]	牙醫
start [start]	啟動（車子）
hurt [hɝt]	痛
break [brek]	動 打破
mad [mæd]	生氣

Life English

MEMO

英文高手教你，居家生活英語

1 起床囉！

美國人怎麼說，我們也跟著說

**要說流利的英語，
從起床那一刻就說英語**

叫起床
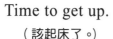

Time to get up.
（該起床了。）

Are you up yet?
（你起來了沒有？）

Wake up.
（醒來。）

I'm already awake.
（我已經醒了。）

Is it time to get up?
（起床的時間到了嗎？）

Is it time already?
（是起床的時間了嗎？）

Okay. I'm getting up.
（好的，我這就起床了。）

I don't want to get up.
（我不想起床。）

I'm still sleepy.
（我還很睏。）

Do I have to?
（我必須起床嗎？）

早上問安

Good morning!
（早安。）

說英語就是這麼簡單

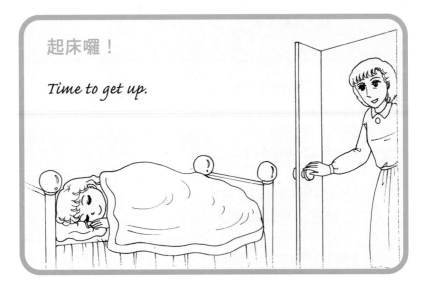

起床囉！

Time to get up.

1. A: Good morning, it's time to get up.
（早安，該起床了。）

B: Let me sleep.
（讓我繼續睡。）

2. A: Good morning. Get out of bed!
（早安，起床了。）

B: You wake me up too early.
（你太早叫我了。）

3. A: John, it's nearly eight o'clock. Get up.
（約翰，快八點了，起床囉。）

B: Oh my gosh. I am late.
（噢，我的天啊，我遲到了。）

4. A: You'd better be getting up now.
（你最好現在就起床。）

It's getting very late.
（很晚了。）

You still have to get ready.
（你還得梳洗呢。）

B: No, it will take me five minutes.
（沒關係，梳洗只要五分鐘就行了。）

實用會話

A: Come on. You need to get up.
（起來吧，你該起床了。）

B: Can't I sleep a little longer?
（我不可以再多睡一會兒嗎？）

A: It's already eight o'clock.
（已經八點了。）

You need to get moving.
（你需要起來了。）

B: All right. I'm getting up.
（好吧，我這就起來。）

sleep [slip]	動 睡覺
nearly [`nɪrlɪ]	幾乎
already [ɔl`rɛdɪ]	副 已經

2 早晨起床後，上廁所

美國人怎麼說，我們也跟著說

要說流利的英語，
起床後上廁所也要說英語

起床後，使用浴室

I have to use the bathroom.
（我要上廁所。）

Did you go to the bathroom?
（你上過廁所了嗎？）

Did you remember to flush?
（你有沒有沖水？）

He needs in the bathroom.

（他需要上廁所。）

Can I get in the bathroom yet?

（我可以上廁所了嗎？）

急著要用廁所

I've really got to go bad!

（我真的很急著要上廁所。）

小孩子要上廁所，所使用的英語

I need to pee.

（我要小便。）

I need to go potty.

（我要去上廁所。）

I need to use the bathroom.

（我要上廁所。）

說英語就是這麼簡單

我要小便

I need to pee.

1. A: Where are you going?
（你要去哪裡？）

B: To the bathroom.
（去廁所。）

I have to pee.
（我要小便。）

2. A: Are you going to be in there long?
（你要用很久嗎？）

B: For a little while.
（一會兒。）

I'm using the bathroom.
（我要上廁所。）

3. A: I'll be back.
（我馬上回來。）

I have to pee.
（我要小便。）

B: I thought you already did.
（我以為你已經去過了。）

4. 小孩：I need to pee.
（我要小便。）

媽媽：I'll help you go to the potty.
（我帶你去坐尿桶。）

小孩：I'm done.
（我小便完了。）

媽媽：Good. Now wash your hands.
（很好，去洗手。）

 實用會話

A：Does anyone need in the bathroom?
（有誰需要用浴室嗎？）

B：I need to pee.
（我要小便。）

A：Then hurry up so I can take my shower.
（那就快點，我要洗淋浴。）

B：Okay, just give me a few seconds.
（好的，給我一點時間。）

It won't take very long.
（不會很久的。）

bathroom [ˈbæθˌrum]	浴室；廁所
remember [rɪˈmɛmbɚ]	記得
flush [flʌʃ]	沖水
really [ˈrɪəlɪ]	真的
pee [pi]	小便
potty [ˈpɑti]	夜壺
thought [θɔt]	想（think 的過去式）；認為
shower [ˈʃaʊɚ]	淋浴

3　早晨起床後，刷牙洗臉

美國人怎麼說，我們也跟著說

要說流利的英語，
起床後刷牙洗臉，
也要說英語

洗臉

Can I come in and wash my face?
（我可以進來洗臉嗎？）

I haven't even washed my face yet.
（我甚至於還沒洗臉呢。）

I just want to wash my face.
（我只是想洗臉。）

Wash your face, you'll feel better.
（洗把臉，你會覺得好一點。）

刷牙

My mouth tastes nasty. I need to brush my teeth.
（我的嘴好臭，我需要去刷牙。）

I've already brushed my teeth.
（我已經刷過牙了。）

Where's the toothbrush?
（牙刷在哪裡？）

Your breath stinks. You need to brush your teeth.
（你的嘴好臭，你需要去刷牙。）

I haven't brushed my teeth yet; I know my breath
stinks.
（我還沒刷牙，我知道我的嘴很臭。）

刮鬍子

Come on in; I'm just shaving.
（進來吧，我只是在刮鬍鬚。）

I need in there so I can shave.
（我需用浴室，我要刮鬍鬚。）

化妝

Have you seen my lipstick?

（你有沒有看到我的唇膏？）

Do I have time to put on make-up?

（我有沒有時間化妝？）

Let me know when you're done shaving so I can put my make-up on.

（你刮完鬍鬚，跟我說一聲，我要化妝。）

I've still got to put my make-up on.

（我還需要化妝。）

Let me finish putting on my make-up and I'll be right out.

（讓我化好妝，我馬上出來。）

在浴室裡，梳洗或上廁所

I need to take a shower.

（我需要洗個淋浴。）

I'm washing my face.

（我在洗臉。）

I'm using the bathroom.
（我在上廁所。）

在浴室裡

I can't find the soap.
（我找不到肥皂。）

Where's my toothbrush?
（我的牙刷在哪裡？）

Where's the soap?
（肥皂在哪裡？）

We don't have any soap.
（肥皂用完了。）

I need a towel.
（我需要一條毛巾。）

Can you hand me the brush? I can't reach it.
（請拿梳子給我。我拿不到。）

Can you pass me the shaving lotion?
（請把刮鬍膏遞給我。）

用玩廁所之後

I forgot to flush.
（我忘了沖水。）

Don't forget to flush.
（別忘了沖水。）

Don't forget to wash your hands.
（別忘了洗手。）

媽媽叮嚀小孩子

Brush your teeth.
（要刷牙。）

Did you wash your face?
（你有沒有洗臉？）

Don't get the water too hot.
（水不要放的太熱。）

Wash behind your ears.
（耳朵後面要記得洗。）

說英語就是這麼簡單

我找不要肥皂

I can't find the soap.

說英語就是這麼簡單

1. A: I'm still sleepy.
（我還是很睏。）

B: Wash your face.
（去洗把臉。）

You'll feel better.
（你會好一點。）

2. A: I need to brush my teeth when you're done.
（你用完後，我要刷牙。）

　　B: Okay, I'll be right out.
（好的，我馬上出來。）

3. A: What's taking you so long in there?
（你怎麼在裡面那麼久？）

　　B: I'm trying to shave.
（我在刮鬍子。）

4. A: Are you finished in there yet?
（你用完了嗎？）

　　B: No, I'm putting on my make-up.
（還沒，我在化妝。）

實用會話

A: I'm going to take my shower.
（我要去洗個淋浴。）

B: All right but try to hurry.
（好的，但是要快一點。）

A: Why? Aren't you already dressed?
（幹嘛！你不是已經穿好衣服了？）

B: I still have to put on my make-up and brush my teeth.
（我還得化妝，還要刷牙。）

mouth [mauθ]	嘴巴
nasty [`næstɪ]	難聞的
brush [brʌʃ]	動 刷
teeth [tiθ]	牙齒

toothbrush [`tuθ͵brʌʃ]	牙刷
stink [stɪŋk]	動 發出惡臭
shaving [`ʃevɪŋ]	刮鬍鬚;shave 的現在分詞
shave [ʃev]	刮鬍鬚
lipstick [`lɪp͵stɪk]	唇膏
make-up [`mek͵ʌp]	化妝品
finish [`fɪnɪʃ]	完成
soap [sop]	名 肥皂
towel [`tauəl]	毛巾
hand [hænd]	動 遞
reach [ritʃ]	拿得到
lotion [`loʃən]	乳液
pass [pæs]	遞
behind [bɪ`haɪnd]	在～的後面
sleepy [`slipɪ]	愛睡的,睏的
hurry [`hɝɪ]	匆忙;趕快

4　穿衣服

美國人怎麼說，我們也跟著說

要說流利的英語，
梳洗完後，
穿衣服，
也要說英語

挑選今天要穿的衣服

What should I wear today?
（我今天應該穿什麼？）

Which one do you like, the green or the purple?
（你喜歡哪一件，綠色還是紫色？）

Should I wear this instead?
（我應該穿這一件，而不要穿那一件嗎？）

What do you think of this sweater?
（這一件毛衣你覺得怎麼樣？）

Don't wear that shirt; it has a stain.

（不要穿那件襯衫，襯衫上有污點。）

I want to wear my blue dress.

（我要穿我的藍色洋裝。）

挑選其他配件

Do these shoes go with this dress?

（這雙鞋子跟這件洋裝相配嗎？）

Which tie should I wear?

（我該戴那一條領帶？）

Does this shirt match this skirt?

（這件襯衫配這件裙子嗎？）

Can you help me pick out a tie?

（你可以幫我挑一條領帶嗎？）

找乾淨，燙過的衣物穿

Are these pants clean?

（這件褲子乾淨嗎？）

I can't wear that; it needs to be ironed.
（我不能穿那件，那件需要用熨斗燙。）

找不到要穿的衣物

Have you seen my tie?
（你有沒有看到我的領帶？）

Did you see where I put my hose?
（你有沒有看要我的褲襪？）

Do you happen to know where my dress is?
（你知不知道我的洋裝放在哪裡？）

告訴找不到衣物的對方，衣物放在哪裡

I think your shirt is hanging in the bathroom.
（我想你的襯衫是掛在浴室裡。）

商借衣物

I ripped my hose. Do you have any I can borrow?

（我勾破我的褲襪，你可以借我一雙嗎？）

穿衣服遇到麻煩

Can you help me button this?

（你可以幫我釦這個鈕釦嗎？）

I'm stuck!

（我卡住了。）

I can't get my arms through.

（我的手伸不過去。）

This zipper's stuck.

（拉鍊卡住了。）

說英語就是這麼簡單

我被卡住了

I'm stuck.

1. A: I can't find my green shirt.

（我找不到我的綠色襯衫。）

B: It's in the wash.

（我拿去洗了。）

Wear the blue one instead.

（穿藍色那一件吧。）

2. A: Have you seen my tie?
（你有沒有看到我的領帶？）

B: Yes. Try looking in your drawer.
（有，到你櫃子的抽屜找找看。）

3. A: Which of these dresses should I wear?
（這幾件洋裝，我應該穿哪一件？）

B: I think the red one looks nice on you.
（我認為紅色那一件你穿起來最好看。）

4. A: Do I have any clean socks?
（有沒有乾淨的襪子我可以穿？）

B: You should.
（應該有。）

I did laundry last night.
（我昨晚洗衣服了。）

實用會話

A: What are you looking for?
（你在找什麼？）

B: My new shirt.
（我的新襯衫。）

The pink one.
（粉紅色的那一件。）

A: I think I saw it hanging in the bathroom.
（我想，我有看到那件掛在浴室裡。）

B: I must've already taken it in there.
（我一定是把它拿進來放在那裡了。）

Thanks.
（謝謝。）

wear [wɛr]	動 穿；戴
purple [`pɝp!]	紫色
instead [ɪn`stɛd]	不是…而是…

sweater [`swɛtɚ]	毛衣
stain [sten]	污點
tie [taɪ]	領帶
match [mætʃ]	動 相配
shirt [ʃɝt]	襯衫
skirt [skɝt]	裙子
pants [pænts]	褲子
iron [`aɪɚn]	用熨斗燙衣服
hose [hoz]	褲襪
hang [hæŋ]	掛
rip [rɪp]	勾破
borrow [`baro]	動 借用
button [`bʌtn]	動 用釦子釦
stuck [stʌk]	卡住
zipper [`zɪpɚ]	拉鍊
drawer [`drɔɚ]	抽屜
clean [klin]	清潔的
sock [sak]	襪子
laundry [`lɔndrɪ]	動 洗衣服

5 吃早餐

美國人怎麼說，我們也跟著說

**要說流利的英語，
吃早餐時，
也要說英語**

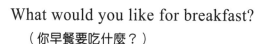

問對方，早餐要吃什麼

What would you like for breakfast?
（你早餐要吃什麼？）

Would you like milk or juice?
（你要喝牛奶還是果汁？）

Do you want cereal for breakfast?
（你要不要吃麥片做早餐？）

Do you want hot tea or coffee with breakfast?

（你早餐要喝熱茶還是咖啡？）

問早餐有什麼可以吃

Isn't there anything here we can eat for breakfast?

（有什麼可以當做早餐吃？）

I'm starving; what's for breakfast?

（我餓死了。早餐吃什麼？）

What's for breakfast?

（早餐吃什麼？）

How about French toast？

（要不要吃法國土司？）

不吃早餐了

Don't bother making breakfast; I'm running late.

（不要做早餐了，我快遲到了。）

I don't have time for breakfast today.

（我今天沒有時間吃早餐。）

I think I'll just skip breakfast.
（我想，我早餐就不吃了。）

煮咖啡，喝牛奶

Do you want me to make some coffee?
（你要不要我泡咖啡？）

Put the coffee on and I'll start breakfast.
（開始泡咖啡，我要吃早餐了。）

Is there any more milk?
（有沒有牛奶？）

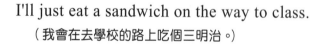

上班上學的路上，吃早餐

I'll just eat a sandwich on the way to class.
（我會在去學校的路上吃個三明治。）

We can pick up breakfast on our way to work.
（我們可以在去上班的路上買個早餐吃。）

叮嚀要吃早餐

Breakfast is ready!
（早餐好了。）

Don't you want some breakfast?
（你不吃早餐嗎？）

You've got to eat some breakfast.
（你早餐一定要吃一點。）

什麼樣的早餐

I'm in the mood for a big breakfast.
（我想吃一頓豐盛的早餐。）

說英語就是這麼簡單

早餐吃什麼？

What's for breakfast?

1. A: Aren't you going to eat any breakfast?
（你不吃早餐嗎？）

B: No thanks. I don't have time.
（不吃，謝謝，我沒有時間。）

2. A: Are you hungry this morning?
（你今天早上餓嗎？）

B: Kind of. Just make me an egg.
（有一點，煮個蛋給我就行。）

3. A: I'm in a hurry.
（我沒時間了。）

I'm running late.
（我快遲到了。）

B: Well, eat a piece of toast or something.
（那，吃片土司麵包，或什麼的。）

4. A: What's for breakfast?
（早餐吃什麼？）

B: How about French toast?
（要吃法國土司麵包嗎？）

A: What do you want for breakfast?
（你早餐要吃什麼？）

B: I'm late.
（我遲到了。）

I really don't have time to eat.
（我真的沒有時間吃了。）

A: You need to eat something.
（你一定得吃點東西。）

How about some toast?
（吃一點土司麵包好嗎？）

B: Some toast will be fine.
（吃一點土司麵包可以。）

 應用會話一

A: What's for breakfast?
（早餐吃什麼？）

B: How about French toast?

（吃法國土司好不好？）

A: That sounds good!

（好啊。）

B: Have a seat and I'll make you some.

（請坐，我做一些給你。）

應用會話二

A: What would you like for breakfast?

（你早餐想吃什麼？）

B: An egg and toast would be fine.

（一個蛋，和一片土司就可以了。）

A: Would you like orange juice or milk with that?

（你要柳橙汁還是牛奶？）

B: Juice, please.

（請給我柳橙汁。）

cereal [`sɪrɪəl]	麥片
milk [mɪlk]	牛奶
juice [dʒus]	果汁
toast [tost]	土司麵包
skip [skɪp]	略過
sandwich [`sændwɪtʃ]	三明治
mood [mud]	心情

6 準備去上班、上學

美國人怎麼說，我們也跟著說

要說流利的英語，
早上出門時，
也要說英語

我要去上班了

I'm off to work.
（我要去上班了。）

I'm leaving now.
（我要走了。）

It's time to go.
（走的時間到了。）

I've got to go.

（我得走了。）

I'd better get going; I'm running late.

（我最好趕快走，否則我會遲到。）

I'd better get a move on or I'll be late.

（我最好趕快動身，否則我會遲到。）

I'm gonna take off now.

（我現在要走了。）

I've got to get to work; I'll call you later.

（我要去上班了，我稍後再打電話給你。）

Okay, I'm heading out.

（好了，我要走了。）

I'm going now; I'll be home late.

（我要走了，我會晚點回來。）

催對方快去上班

You're going to be late.

（你會遲到的。）

Get going. You don't want to be late.

（快走，你不想遲到的。）

You'd better get moving. You've got ten minutes to get to work.

（你最好快走，你還有十分鐘就要上班。）

 再見

I'll see you later.

（再見。）

I'll see you after work.

（下班後再見。）

I'm taking off but I'll see you at lunch.

（我要走了，午餐時再見。）

See you tonight.

（今晚見。）

對方上班前，你叮嚀對方

Be careful, the traffic is pretty bad.
（小心點，交通很不好。）

Call me at the office if you need anything.
（如果你需要什麼東西，到了辦公司再打電話給我。）

When will you be back tonight?
（你今晚什麼時候回來？）

Have a good day and I'll see you later.
（祝你一天愉快，再見。）

說英語就是這麼簡單

校車來了！

Here comes the bus.

1. A: Oh my gosh! It's already nine.
（天啊，已經九點了。）

B: You'd better head out or you'll be late.
（你最好快出門，否則你會遲到。）

2. A: I'd better get going.
（我該走了。）

B: I'll see you this evening.
（今晚再見。）

Have a good day.
（祝你一天愉快。）

3. A: I'll see you tonight.
（今天晚上見。）

Tell the kids bye for me.
（跟孩子們說再見。）

B: Okay. See you then.
（好的，再見。）

4. A: Shouldn't you be off to work?
（你不是該去上班了嗎？）

B: You're right.
（是啊。）

I'd better get a move on.
（我得走了。）

·················· 實用會話 ··················

A: I'm off to work.
　（我要去上班了。）

B: Are you leaving already?
　（你現在就要走了？）

A: Yes, I have twenty minutes to get there.
　（是啊，我還有二十分鐘就到上班時間了。）

B: Gosh. I didn't realize it was that late.
　（天啊，我不曉得已經那麼晚了。）

 ·················· 應用會話一 ··················

A: I'm off to work.
　（我要去上班了。）

B: Will you be home for lunch?
　（你要回來吃午飯嗎？）

A:Probably not but I should be home early tonight.

（可能不回來吃午飯，但是我晚上會早一點回來。）

B: Okay, I'll see you then.

（好的，再見。）

Have a nice day.

（祝你一天愉快。）

later [ˋletɚ]	稍後
head [hɛd]	動 朝特定方向行進
traffic [ˋtræfɪk]	交通
pretty [ˋprɪtɪ]	副 非常；相當
careful [ˋkɛrfəl]	小心；仔細的
realize [ˋrɪəˌlaɪz]	明瞭；知道
probably [ˋprɑbəblɪ]	或許；可能的

124

7 午餐時間

美國人怎麼說，我們也跟著說

要說流利的英語，
吃午餐時，
也要說英語

相約去吃午餐

Do you want some lunch?
（你要不要吃午飯？）

Do you want to go to lunch?
（你要不要去吃午飯？）

Should we grab a bite to eat?
（我們是否該買個東西吃？）

Let's go to lunch.
（去吃午飯吧。）

Meet me at the cafe. We'll have lunch.
（在小餐館等我，我們一起吃午飯。）

I'm going to Juan's for lunch if you want to come?
（我要去吉安餐廳吃午飯，你要不要一起來？）

How about going to Jason's for lunch?
（去傑森餐廳吃午飯好不好？）

 回家吃午餐

I'm coming home for lunch.
（我會回來吃午飯。）

Will you be home for lunch?
（你會回來吃午飯嗎？）

126

午餐吃什麼

This smells great! What's for lunch?
（好香，午飯吃什麼？）

Is there anything special you want for lunch?
（你中午有沒有特別想吃什麼？）

I think I want hot and sour soup for lunch.
（我中午想喝酸辣湯。）

I'm in the mood for French, how about you?
（我想吃法國食物，你呢？）

Have we decided what we're going to do about lunch yet?
（我們決定好，要去哪裡吃午飯了嗎？）

Let's have Italian for lunch.
（我們中午吃義大利食物吧。）

Do you want hamburgers for lunch?
（你中午想不想吃漢堡？）

We're ordering Jason's for lunch. Do you want anything?
（我們要到傑森餐廳叫菜，你要吃什麼嗎？）

 請吃午飯

It's my turn to pay for lunch.

（這次輪到我請吃午飯。）

Come on, I'll buy you lunch.

（來吧，我請你吃午飯。）

I want to take you to lunch.

（我請你去吃午飯。）

I'll buy you lunch today if you buy tomorrow.

（如果你明天請吃午飯的話，今天午飯我請客。）

Oh, how sweet! You brought me lunch.

（噢，好棒，你帶了午飯給我。）

Let's go to lunch, my treat.

（去吃午飯吧，我請客。）

 午餐時間到了

Is it lunchtime yet?

（午餐時間到了沒有？）

Come on, it's time for lunch.

（來吧，午飯時間到了。）

I'm going to take a long lunch.

（我中午會吃久一點。）

I hope it's time for lunch soon. I'm starving.

（我希望午餐時間快到，我快餓死了。）

It's lunchtime.

（是午餐時間到了。）

不吃午飯

I've got too much work to do. I'm going to have to skip lunch.

（我有太多事情要做，我午餐不吃了。）

I have to eat quick today. I've got a meeting in less than an hour.

（我今天要吃得很快，一小時之內，我有會議要開。）

吃過飯沒有

Have you had lunch today?

（你吃過午飯了嗎？）

I'm not hungry yet.

（我還不餓。）

I've already eaten.

（我吃過了。）

說英語就是這麼簡單

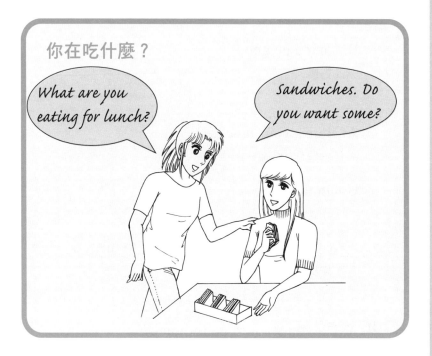

你在吃什麼？

What are you eating for lunch?

Sandwiches. Do you want some?

1. A: What's for lunch?
（午餐吃什麼？）

I'm starved.
（我餓死了。）

B: I was thinking of hamburgers.
（我在想，吃漢堡怎麼樣。）

2. A: Do you want to order a pizza for lunch?
（你午餐要叫匹薩餅來吃嗎？）

B: That'd be good.
（好啊。）

3. A: Here's your lunch.
（這是你的午餐。）

B: Oh thanks.
（謝謝。）

It was nice of you to bring it to me.
（謝謝你拿過來給我。）

4. A: Do you want to go to lunch?
（你要去吃午餐嗎？）

B: Yeah. That would be great.
（好啊。）

A: Do you want to have lunch together?
（你要不要跟我一起去吃午飯？）

B: That would be good.
（好啊。）

I get off in about twenty minutes.
（我差不多二十分，就可以走了。）

A: Okay.
（好的。）

I'll finish this up and meet you outside.
（我把這個做完，在外面等你。）

B: Great.
（好。）

I'll see you then.
（待會兒見。）

應用會話一

A: Do you want some lunch?
（你要不要吃午飯？）

B: Sure, what are you having?
（可以，你有什麼可以吃的？）

A: I can't decide between soup or a salad.
（我不知道要煮湯還是弄些沙拉？）

B: I think a salad would be great.
（我想沙拉好了。）

應用會話二

A: What are you eating for lunch?
（你中午要吃什麼？）

B: Leftovers.
（剩菜。）

Do you want some?
（你要不要吃一些？）

A: No thanks. I'm not hungry.

（不用，謝謝，我不餓。）

B: Are you sure?

（真的？）

A: Yeah, I've already eaten.

（是啊，我已經吃過了。）

B: Okay, suit yourself.

（好吧，隨便你。）

grab [græb]	匆忙地拿；隨便吃一下
bite [baɪt]	名 一口；簡單的飲食
cafe [kə`fe]	小餐館；咖啡館
smell [smɛl]	動 聞到；聞起來
special [`spɛʃəl]	特別的
mood [mud]	心情

soup [sup]	湯
sour [`saʊr]	酸的
hot [hɑt]	辣的
decide [dɪ`saɪd]	動 決定；判斷
hamburger [`hæmbɚgɚ]	漢堡
order [`ɔrdɚ]	動 點菜
turn [tɝn]	輪流
pay [pe]	付錢
treat [trit]	動 請客
skip [skɪp]	跳過
meet [mit]	見面
outside [`aʊt`saɪd]	外面
leftovers [`lɛftovɚ]	剩菜

8　回家了

美國人怎麼說，我們也跟著說

要說流利的英語，
回家時，
也要說英語

我回家了

Hey, I'm home.
（嗨，我回來了。）

I'm back.
（我回來了。）

家人下班，放學回來，你問候他

How was your day?
（你今天好嗎？）

So, tell me about your day.
（告訴我，你今天都做了什麼事。）

Are you glad to be back home?
（回到了家，你高興嗎？）

You look tired.
（你看起來累了。）

I didn't expect you back so soon.
（我沒想到你會那麼早回來。）

Back already?
（你回來了？）

How did it go today?
（今天怎麼樣？）

What happened at school?
（今天學校裡，怎麼樣？）

How did the meeting go?

（會議開得怎麼樣？）

回家了，真好

What a long day, I'm glad I'm finally home.

（今天真忙，我很高興終於回家了。）

I had such a long day; I'm completely exhausted.

（今天夠忙的，我累壞了。）

Traffic was awful; it took me an hour just to get home.

（交通好擁擠，要一個小時才到得了家。）

It feels good to be back home.

（回家真好。）

說今天的情形

I had a terrible day.

（今天很糟。）

I had fun today.
（我今天玩得很好。）

回家後，問候在家裡的家人

Did anything happen while I was at work?
（我在公司的時候，家裡有什麼事？）

What did you do today?
（你今天做什麼？）

140

說英語就是這麼簡單

你一整天都好嗎？

Time to get up.

I had fun today.

How was your day?

1. A: Mary, is that you?
（瑪麗，是你嗎？）

B: Yeah, it's me.
（是的，是我。）

I just got in.
（我剛進來。）

2. A: Mary, I'm home.
（瑪麗，我回來了。）

B: How was your day?
（你今天好嗎？）

3. A: Hey guys.
（嗨，各位。）

B: You're back already?
（你回來了？）

Today sure went fast.
（今天過得真快。）

4. A: How was your day, honey?
（親愛的，你今天好嗎？）

B: Pretty good.
（很好。）

How was yours?
（你呢，你今天怎麼樣？）

實用會話

A: Is that you, John?
（約翰，是你嗎？）

B: Yeah. It's me.
（是的，是我。）

A: I didn't expect you back so soon.
（我沒想到你會這麼早回來。）

B: Well, I finished up early today.
（嗯，我今天的工作早一點做完。）

 應用會話一

A: How was work today?
（今天在公司怎麼樣？）

B: We were pretty busy.
（今天很忙。）

A: Did you make a lot of sales?
（你有沒有做成很多生意？）

B: As a matter of fact, I did.

（事實上，我是做成很多筆生意。）

A: That's great!

（那很棒。）

tired [taɪrd]	疲倦的
expect [ɪk`spɛkt]	預期；期待
happen [`hæpən]	發生
meeting [`mitɪŋ]	會議
finally [`faɪn̩lɪ]	最終；終於
exhausted [ɪg`zɔstɪd]	筋疲力盡
completely [kəm`plitlɪ]	完全地
awful [`ɔfʊl]	動 很糟的
terrible [`tɛrəbḷ]	（口語）糟透的
fun [fʌn]	好玩；樂趣
fast [fæst]	快
busy [`bɪzɪ]	忙的
sales [selz]	銷售

144

9 晚餐

美國人怎麼說，我們也跟著說

要説流利的英語，
吃晚飯時，
也要説英語

 要吃飯了

I guess I should start dinner.
（我想該吃晚飯了。）

What's for dinner?
（晚餐吃什麼？）

I'm starving, is dinner ready yet?
（我快餓死了，晚餐好了沒有？）

It's suppertime!

（吃晚飯了。）

It's time to eat.

（吃飯了。）

Is dinner ready yet?

（晚飯好了沒有？）

 晚餐快好了

Dinner is almost ready. I hope you're hungry.

（晚飯快好了。我希望你肚子餓了。）

Dinner's just about ready.

（晚飯快好了。）

準備吃飯

Can you set the table for me?

（請你幫我準備碗筷。）

Dinner is ready.

（晚飯好了。）

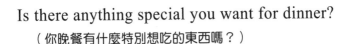

你晚餐想吃什麼

Is there anything special you want for dinner?

（你晚餐有什麼特別想吃的東西嗎？）

Why don't we go out for dinner?

（我們何不出去吃晚餐？）

Let's order out.

（我們叫外賣吧。）

Are you ready for dinner?

（你們要吃晚飯了嗎？）

What are you hungry for?

（你要吃什麼？）

今晚的晚餐

We're having baked fish for dinner.

（我們今晚吃烤魚。）

What do you think about fried chicken for
dinner?

（晚餐吃炸雞，你們認為如何？）

Do you want me to make a salad for dinner?
（晚餐你們要我做沙拉嗎？）

Should we have peas for dinner or corn?
（我們晚餐該吃豌豆還是玉米？）

I think you should make cabbage for dinner.
（我認為你該煮高麗菜做晚飯。）

Try this. It's a new recipe.
（試試看，是新的食譜。）

Guess what I made for dinner?
（猜猜看，我晚飯煮什麼？）

真好吃

This is really good. What's it called?
（這道菜真好吃，叫什麼名字？）

Dinner was great!
（晚餐真棒。）

I don't like pork but the vegetables are really good.
（我不喜歡豬肉，但是蔬菜很好吃。）

What did you put in this? I really like it!

（你裡面放了什麼東西，我喜歡吃。）

Oh, you made shrimp! My favorite!

（噢，你做了蝦子，是我最喜歡吃的。）

再來一碗

If you want seconds, there's plenty left.

（你如果還要再來一碗，還有很多。）

May I have seconds?

（我可以再來一碗嗎？）

Does anyone want seconds?

（有沒有人要再來一碗？）

我飽了

I'm full.

（我飽了。）

Are you still hungry?

（你還餓嗎？）

Do you want any more?
（你還要嗎？）

飯後甜點

Do you want some dessert?
（你要不要來些甜點？）

I've got some ice cream if you're still hungry
after dinner.
（吃了晚餐，如果你還餓的話，我有一些冰淇淋。）

別客氣

Help yourself.
（別客氣。）

說英語就是這麼簡單

不，我飽了。

No, I'm full.

1. A: Do you want anything special for dinner?

（你今晚有沒有特別想吃什麼？）

B: Whatever you make will be fine.

（你煮什麼都好。）

2. A: Come on in. It's time to eat.
（進來吧，吃飯時間到了。）

B: Great. What's for dinner?
（很好，晚餐吃什麼？）

3. A: Should I make dinner?
（我該去做晚飯了嗎？）

B: To tell you the truth, I'm not really hungry.
（說實話，我還不太餓。）

4. A: What are we doing for dinner tonight?
（我們今天晚餐要做什麼？）

B: I think we're having dinner with your parents.
（我想，我們是要跟你的父母一起吃晚飯。）

A: I'm starving!

（我餓死了。）

B: Hold on.

（忍著點。）

Dinner's almost ready.

（晚飯快好了。）

A: What are we having?

（我們今晚吃什麼？）

It smells good.

（聞起來好香。）

B: I'm making that baked fish that you like so
much.

（我在煮你最喜歡吃的烤魚。）

應用會話一

A: What's for supper?
（晚餐吃什麼？）

B: I'm making roast beef.
（我在做烤牛肉。）

A: That sounds really good.
（聽起來不錯。）

I'm starving.
（我快餓死了。）

B: Well, go wash your hands.
（那，去洗手。）

It's almost ready.
（快好了。）

 應用會話二

A: Supper was delicious.
（晚餐真好吃。）

B: There's more if you want seconds.

（如果你還要再來一碗，還有。）

A: No, thanks.

（不用了，謝謝你。）

I've eaten enough.

（我吃飽了。）

B: Me too.

（我也是。）

I'm so full. I'm about to pop.

（我吃的好飽，簡直要撐死了。）

guess [gɛs]	猜想
ready [ˋrɛdɪ]	準備好
almost [ˋɔlˏmost]	副 幾乎
baked [bekt]	烤的

fried [fraɪd]	炸的
recipe [ˋrɛsəpɪ]	食譜
pork [pork]	豬肉
vegetable [ˋvɛdʒətəbl]	蔬菜
shrimp [ʃrɪmp]	蝦
favorite [ˋfevərɪt]	最喜歡的
seconds [ˋsɛkəndz]	第二碗
plenty [ˋplɛntɪ]	很多
left [lɛft]	剩下的
full [fʊl]	吃飽
dessert [dɪˋzɝt]	名（飯後）甜點
roast [rost]	烤
beef [bif]	牛肉
delicious [dɪˋlɪʃəs]	形 好吃的；美味的
pop [pɑp]	爆裂
enough [əˋnʌf]	足夠的

10 起床囉！

美國人怎麼說，我們也跟著說

**要說流利的英語，
看電視時也要說英語**

有什麼好看的電視節目

Is there anything good on tonight?
（今晚有什麼好看的節目？）

What's on the tube?
（電視上有什麼節目？）

What's on TV tonight?
（今晚電視上有什麼節目？）

某個電視節目

Does my show come on tonight or tomorrow?

（我要看的節目，是今晚還是明天播映？）

I think we missed our show.

（我想我們沒看到我們要看的節目。）

Damn! I missed the beginning of it.

（真是的，我沒看到這個節目的開始。）

This is a good show. I'd like to see the whole thing some time.

（這個節目很好，有空我想看整個節目。）

We'll have to try to catch it next time it's on.

（這個節目下次播映的時候，我們一定要看。）

Do you know when this show will be on again?

（你知不知道，這個節目下次什麼時候播映？）

I love this show! I watch it everytime it comes on.

（我喜歡這個節目，每次播映我都有看。）

This show seems to drag on forever. I'm tired of it already.

（這個節目，拖個沒完，我真是煩死了。）

看電視

What are you watching?

（你在看什麼？）

There's nothing good on tonight.

（今晚沒什麼好看的節目。）

Why do you always watch reruns?

（你為什麼總是看重播節目？）

Is there anything new on TV tonight?

（今晚有沒有什麼新的節目？）

There's nothing on. We should just rent a movie.

（沒什麼好看的節目，我們應該去租部電影。）

Have you ever seen this show before?

（你以前有沒有看過這個節目？）

What are you watching? That's the strangest thing I've ever seen!

（你在看什麼，那是我看過最奇怪的東西。）

I've got to go to the bathroom, tell me what I miss.

（我要去上廁所，我沒看到的部分，你要告訴我。）

I think I've seen this show before.

（我想我以前看過這個節目。）

看有沒有其他節目

What else is on?

（還有什麼其他的節目？）

不要看這個節目

I've already seen this.

（這個節目我已經看過了。）

Please don't make me watch that stupid show again.

（請你不要再叫我看那個蠢節目。）

This is one of the worst movies ever made.

（這是最爛的電影。）

Can I see what else is on?

（我可不可以看看還有什麼其他的節目？）

The kids probably shouldn't watch this show.

（小孩子可能不應該看這個節目。）

I can't stand to watch shows like this.

（像這樣的節目，我看不下去。）

看新聞

See if the news is on. I want to catch the weather.

（看看是不是在播報新聞，我想看氣象預告。）

這個節目好不好要看

Is that a good show?
（那個節目好嗎？）

I really think you'll like this show.
（我真的認為你會喜歡這個節目。）

換個電視台

Do you mind if I change the channel?
（我如果換到其他電視台你會介意嗎？）

Is it all right if I change the channel?
（我可以換到其他電視台嗎？）

See what's on channel 43.
（看看 43 台在播映什麼？）

Let's watch something funny.
（我們看喜劇片吧。）

I wonder if there are any scary movies on.
（我不知道有沒有恐怖片在上演。）

Which channel does that movie come on?
（那一部電影在哪一台播映？）

說英語就是這麼簡單

有什麼節目可以看

What's on TV tonight?

Nothing much. Just a bunch of reruns.

1. A: Is there anything good on?
（有沒有什麼好的節目？）

B: I think Friends is on tonight.
（我想今天晚上會播歡樂單身派對）

2. A: What are you watching?

（你在看什麼？）

B: I don't know what it's called but it sure is funny.

（我不曉得是什麼節目，但是很有趣。）

3. A: Dinner was great.

（今天晚飯真棒。）

B: Thank you.

（謝謝。）

I'll clear the table and we can watch some TV.

（我要收拾桌子，然後我們可以看一點電視。）

4. A: Do you want to watch anything special tonight?

（你今晚想看什麼節目嗎？）

B: Actually, there's a great movie coming on the sci-fi channel.

（事實上，科幻台有一部很好看的電影要上演。）

實用會話

A: Isn't your movie on tonight?
（你要看的電影不是今晚要放映嗎？）

B: That's right.
（是啊。）

I forgot all about it.
（我全忘了。）

A: Do you know what time it comes on?
（你知道幾點要放映嗎？）

B: I think it's supposed to start around eight.
（我想，應該是八點左右。）

 應用會話一

A: What's on TV tonight?
（今晚電視上有什麼節目？）

B: Nothing much.
（沒什麼。）

Just a bunch of reruns.

（只是一大堆重播節目。）

A: I thought Of Mice and Men was coming on.

（我以為『人與鼠』今晚要播映。）

B: That's not until next week.

（下星期才會播映的。）

應用會話二

A: Is there anything good on tonight?

（今晚電視上有什麼節目？）

B: There is an interesting film on channel 18.

（第 18 台有部很有趣的電影。）

A: Are you going to watch it?

（你要看嗎？）

B: I'm planning to.

（我打算要看。）

A: Can I watch it with you?

（我可以跟你一起看嗎？）

B: Sure, be my guest.

（當然可以，歡迎。）

單字片語

tube [tjub]	名 電視機
show [ʃo]	節目
miss [mɪs]	動 錯過
whole [hol]	全部的；整體的
catch [kætʃ]	趕上
drag [dræg]	拖
forever [fəˋɛvɚ]	永久的
rerun [ˋriˏrʌn]	重播
rent [rɛnt]	出租
strangest [strendʒɪst]	最奇怪的

else [ɛls]	其他的
worst [wɝst]	最壞的
stupid [ˈstjupɪd]	愚；蠢
news [njuz]	新聞
weather [ˈwɛðɚ]	天氣
mind [maɪnd]	動 介意
channel [ˈtʃænḷ]	名（廣播）頻道
funny [ˈfʌnɪ]	滑稽；好笑的
wonder [ˈwʌndɚ]	想；想知道
scary [ˈskɛrɪ]	恐怖的
clear [klɪr]	清理
actually [ˈæktʃʊəlɪ]	副 實際上；事實上
supposed [səˈpozd]	（口語）應該
film [fɪlm]	名 電影
plan [plæn]	計畫

11 看報紙

美國人怎麼說，我們也跟著說

**要說流利的英語，
看電報紙時也要說英語**

報紙拿進來了沒有

Did we get today's paper?

（今天的報紙拿進來了沒有？）

看報紙

Have you read the paper yet today?

（你今天的報紙看過了嗎？）

I've already read the paper today.
（我今天的報紙已經看過了。）

Was there anything interesting in the paper today?
（今天報紙上有沒有什麼有趣的新聞？）

What are you reading about?
（你在看什麼？）

 這條新聞很有趣

I want you to read this article when I'm done.
（我看完後，我要你看這條新聞。）

There's an article I want you to read on page E3.
（E3 那一頁有一個新聞，你一定要看。）

Here, check this out.
（來，看看這條新聞。）

There was a great article in the paper today.
（今天的報紙上有一條大新聞。）

Did you read the article about the monkey?
（你有沒有看到那條有關猴子的新聞？）

This article is so interesting. Listen to this. . .
（這條新聞很有趣，聽著…）

請對方拿某一版給你

Are you finished with the sports section?
（體育版你看完了嗎？）

Can I have the classifieds when you're done?
（你看完之後，請把廣告版拿給我。）

Can I see the paper when you're through with it?
（你看完之後，把報紙給我。）

Hand me the sports section please.
（請把體育版給我。）

拿報紙給對方看

Here, I'm done with this part of the paper.
（拿去，這一部份我看完了。）

I'm almost finished with the paper if you want it.
（如果你要看的話，我快看完了。）

Do you want me to save the paper for you?
（你要我幫你留著報紙嗎？）

I left the paper on the table by your chair.
（我把報紙放在你椅子邊的桌上。）

找某一版的報紙

Save me the paper when you're through.
（你報紙看完後，幫我留著。）

I'm looking for the book reviews.
（我在找書評那一版。）

What page are the editorials on?
（社論在哪一版？）

Do you ever read the Dear Abby column?
（你有沒有看過『親愛的艾琵』專欄？）

I think the entertainment section is missing.

（娛樂版好像不見了。）

看漫畫版

I love the comics.

（我喜歡漫畫。）

The comics were so funny today.

（今天的漫畫真有趣。）

You've got to read the comics.

（這則漫畫你一定要看。）

You're going to crack up when you read Garfield.

你看這篇『加菲貓』漫畫，你一定會笑破肚皮。

說英語就是這麼簡單

看報紙

Reading the newspaper.

What are you doing, Dad?

1. A: Do you want to watch some TV?
（你要看電視嗎？）

B: No thanks.
（不。）

I think I'm going to read the paper.
（我想我要看報紙。）

2. A: I left the paper on the table for you.
（我把報紙放在桌上給你。）

B: Thanks. I think I'll go read it.
（謝謝，我想我會去看看報紙。）

3. A: Are you still reading the paper?
（你還在看報紙嗎？）

B: No. I'm done if you want it.
（沒有，如果你要看的話拿去，我看完了。）

4. A: Could you hand me the business section, please?
（請你把工商版遞給我。）

B: Sure. Here you go.
（好的，在這裡。）

英語高手教你，家居生活英語　175

實用會話

A: Don't throw out the paper.
（別把報紙丟掉。）

I haven't read it yet.
（我還沒看。）

B: I won't.
（我不會丟掉。）

I'm still reading it myself.
（我自己還在看。）

A: Can I see the sports section or are you still reading it?
（可以把體育版給我看嗎，還是你還在看？）

B: No, I'm done.
（不，我已經看完了。）

Here, you can have the comics, too.
（在這兒，漫畫版也順便拿去。）

應用會話一

A: What are you doing, Dad?
（爸爸，你在做什麼？）

B: Reading the newspaper.
（看報紙。）

A: Can I see the classifieds?
（可以把分類廣告給我嗎？）

B: In just a minute.
（稍等一下。）

I'm not done with them yet.
（我還沒看完。）

 應用會話二

A: I read an interesting article in the paper today.
（我在今天的報紙上看到一篇有趣的新聞。）

B: Really?
（真的？）

What was it about?
（是什麼新聞？）

A: It was about the new gorilla exhibit at the zoo.
（是說動物園裡新的猩猩展覽。）

B: I'd like to read it.
（我想讀讀看。）

A: Here's the paper.
（報紙在這裡。）

It is on page 12.
（新聞是在第十二頁。）

B: Thanks.
（謝謝。）

I'll give it back to you when I'm through.
（我看完之後，會還給你。）

paper [`pepɚ]	報紙（newspaper 的簡寫）
article [`ɑrtɪkl̩]	報導

page [pedʒ]	頁
monkey [`mʌŋkɪ]	猴子
listen [`lɪsn]	動 聽；傾聽
sports [spɔrts]	運動
section [`sɛkʃən]	（報紙）版；
classified [`klæsə͵faɪd]	分類廣告
save [sev]	保留
review [rɪ`vju]	審核
editorial [͵ɛdə`tɔrɪəl]	社論
column [`kɑləm]	專欄
entertainment [͵ɛntɚ`tenmənt]	名 娛樂
missing [`mɪsɪŋ]	形 不見了；丟了
comics [`kɑmɪks]	漫畫
business [`bɪznɪs]	名 工商企業；商務
throw [θro]	動 扔掉
exhibit [ɪg`zɪbɪt]	展覽
gorilla [gə`rɪlə]	名 大猩猩
listen to	聽
crack up	笑破肚皮

12 應門

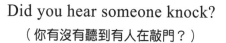
門鈴響了

Did you hear someone knock?
（你有沒有聽到有人在敲門？）

Did the doorbell just ring?
（剛剛是不是有人按門鈴？）

I think someone's at the door.
（好像有人在敲門。）

I thought I heard somebody knocking.

（我好像聽到有人在敲門。）

Is someone at the door?

（有人在敲門嗎？）

有人在敲門，去看看是誰來了

See who's at the door.

（去看看是誰？）

See who it is.

（去看看是誰？）

問家裡面的人，有誰可以去應門

Can somebody please get the door?

（誰有空去應門？）

Could someone get the door?

（誰有空去應門？）

跟門外敲門的人說，我來開門了

Coming.

（我來給你開門了。）

Just a minute! I'll be right there.

（稍等一下，我馬上來。）

跟家裡面的人說，我去應門

I'll get it.

（我就去應門。）

問門外是誰

Who is it?

（是誰啊？）

Who's at the door?

（門外是誰？）

Who's there?

（是誰啊？）

開門後，跟來訪客人說的話

Hey, come on in.
（嗨，請進來。）

What are you doing here?
（有什麼事嗎？）

Come in; come in.
（請進，請進。）

So, what brings you here?
（什麼風把你吹來的？）

 訪客報姓名，說明來意

It's me, John.
（是我，約翰。）

I just wanted to stop by and say hello.
（我只是過來坐一下，打個招呼。）

I was in the neighborhood and I thought I'd stop by.
（我來到這附近，順便過來坐一下。）

Is Mary home?
（瑪麗在家嗎？）

告訴訪客，你會去請訪客要找的人來

Hold on and I'll go get her.
（稍後，我去叫她。）

He's coming.
（他馬上就來。）

She'll be right down.
（她馬上就來。）

He's in the backyard.
（他在後院。）

We've been expecting you.
（我們正在等你。）

He's upstairs. Let me go get him.
（他在樓上，我去叫他。）

告訴家裡的人，有訪客來訪

Mary, you've got company.

（瑪麗，有人要找你。）

FAST & EASY

說英語就是這麼簡單

是誰啊？

Who's there?

It's me, John.

（有人在按門鈴，媽媽問有誰可以去應門）

A: Could someone please get the door?

（誰有空去應門？）

B: I'll get it, mom.

（媽，我去。）

（小孩應門之後，媽媽問是誰？）

A: Who is it?

（是哪位啊 ？）

B: It's Mr. Lin.

（是林先生。）

He wants to talk to you for a minute.

（他要跟你講話。）

A: Tell him I'll be right there.

（告訴他，我馬上就來。）

應用會話一

（在門內問門外是誰）

A: Who's there?

（門外是誰？）

B: It's me, John.

（是我，約翰。）

（知道是誰之後，把門打開）

A: Hi John, come on in.
（嗨，約翰，請進來。）

What brings you here?
（有什麼事嗎？）

B: I was just wondering if Mary wanted to study with me.
（我只是想邀瑪麗跟我一起唸書。）

A: Wait here and I'll go get her.
（稍等一下，我去叫她。）

B: Okay, Mrs. Lin.
（好的，林太太。）

Thanks.
（謝謝。）

knock [nɑk]	敲；敲門
doorbell [`dor͵bɛl]	門鈴
ring [rɪŋ]	動 鈴響
bring [brɪŋ]	動 帶來
neighborhood [`nebɚ͵hʊd]	鄰近地區
backyard [`bækjɑrd]	後院
upstairs [`ʌp`stɛrz]	樓上
company [`kʌmpənɪ]	名 夥伴

13 接電話

美國人怎麼說，我們也跟著說

**要説流利的英語，
聽電話時也要説英語**

 是你的電話

It's for you.
（你的電話。）

Dad, telephone.
（爹，你的電話。）

Mary, John is on the phone.
（瑪麗，約翰打電話來要找你。）

誰有空去接個電話

Can somebody please get the phone?
（誰有空去接個電話？）

我去接電話

I'll get it.
（我去接電話。）

是電話鈴響嗎

Did you hear the phone ringing?
（你有沒有聽到電話鈴響？）

Is that the phone?
（是電話在響嗎？）

看看是誰打來的

See who that is.
（問看看是誰打來的。）

說英語就是這麼簡單

你的電話

1. A: Could somebody get the phone?

（誰去接個電話？）

B: I'll get it.

（我去。）

2. A: John, telephone.

（約翰，你的電話。）

B: Who is it?

（是誰打來的？）

3. A: John, Mary's on the phone.

（約翰，瑪麗打電話來要找你。）

B: Tell her I'm in the shower and I'll call her back.

（告訴她，我在洗澡，我會回她電話。）

4. A: Dad, it's for you.

（爸，是你的電話。）

B: Thank you, Mary.

（謝謝你，瑪麗。）

A:John, Mary's on the phone.
（約翰，瑪麗打電話要找你。）

B:I'm really busy.
（我很忙。）

Ask her if I can call her back.
（跟她說，我再打給她好不好。）

A:Okay but she said it was important.
（好的，但是她說有很重要的事要跟你說。）

B:Fine.
（好的。）

Tell her I'll be right there.
（告訴她，我馬上來。）

 .... 應用會話一 ....

A:Could someone please get the phone?
（誰有空去接個電話？）

My hands are dirty.

（我的手髒。）

B: Don't worry, dad. I'll get it.

（別擔心，爸爸，我去接。）

A: Thanks.

（謝謝。）

If it's for me, find out who it is.

（如果是要找我，問看看是誰。）

Then tell him, I'll call him back.

（然後告訴他，我會打給他。）

B: Okay, dad.

（好的，爸爸。）

No problem.

（沒問題。）

應用會話二

A: Mom, Telephone!

（媽，你的電話。）

B: Who is it?

（是誰打來的？）

A: I don't know.

（我不知道。）

She didn't say, but it sounds like grandma.

（她沒說，但是聽起來好像是外婆。）

B: Okay, tell her to hold on a minute.

（好的，請她等一下。）

I'll be right there.

（我馬上來。）

important [ɪm`pɔrtnt]	形 重要的
dirty [`dɝtɪ]	髒的
worry [`wɝɪ]	動 憂慮；擔心
problem [`prɑbləm]	問題
sound [saʊnd]	動 聽起來

14　睡前

美國人怎麼說，我們也跟著說

**要說流利的英語，
要去洗澡時，
也要說英語**

睡覺前，洗個澡

I really need to take a shower before bed.
（我睡覺前，該去洗個澡。）

A nice, hot bath sounds good right about now.
（現在，洗個熱水澡一定很好。）

I think I'm going to take a bath.
（我想我要去洗澡了。）

Why don't you take a bath? It will help you relax.
（你何不去洗個澡？洗個澡你會舒服一點。）

I'm going to take a shower. Do you need in here first?
（我要去洗淋浴，你要先進來用嗎？）

I had a long day so I'm just going to sit in the tub and relax.
（我今天夠忙的了，我要去泡個熱水，放輕鬆一下。）

I should probably take a shower and get ready for bed.
（我也許該去洗個澡，準備睡覺了。）

I'm going to take a bath. Does anyone need in before I do?
（我要去洗澡了，有沒有人要先用浴室？）

睡覺前，卸妝

I'd better take my make-up off.
（我最好去卸妝。）

Can you hand me my face cream?
（請你把我的乳液遞給我。）

Don't forget to take your make-up off.
（別忘了要卸妝。）

Let me know when you're out so I can take my make-up off.
（你出來的時候，跟我說一聲，我要卸妝。）

I'm too tired to take a shower. I'll just take my make-up off and go to bed.
（我太累了，不洗澡了，我卸了妝，就要去睡覺了。）

Just take your make-up off. You can shower in the morning.
（只要卸妝就好，明天早上再洗澡。）

 換睡衣

These clothes are uncomfortable. I'm going to change into my pj's.
（這些衣服穿起來很不舒服，我要去換睡衣。）

Thanks for washing my pj's, honey.

（親愛的，謝謝你幫我洗睡衣。）

Ahh, that's much better. It feels good to get out of my clothes.

（哈，舒服多了，脫掉衣服覺得好舒服。）

Are my pj's in there?

（我的睡衣在那裡面嗎？）

I'm going to take a bath and change into my pj's.

（我要去洗個澡，然後換上睡衣。）

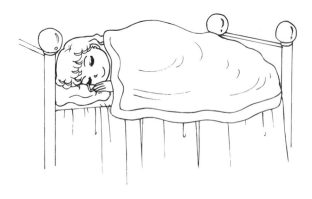

說英語就是這麼簡單

起床囉！

Are you ready for bed?

Not yet.
I still need to take a shower.

1. A: I think I'm going to get ready for bed.
（我想我得準備去睡覺了。）

B: Good idea.
（我想也是。）

Can you hand me my pj's?
（請你把我的睡衣拿給我。）

2. A: I've had such a long day.
（我今天夠忙的。）

B: Why don't you take a bath and get ready for bed?
（你何不去洗個澡，準備睡覺了？）

3. A: Let me know when you're finished.
（你用完之後，告訴我一聲。）

I have to take my make-up off.
（我必須要卸妝。）

B: I'm just going to take a quick shower.
（我只是很快洗個淋浴。）

I'll be right out.
（我馬上出來。）

4. A: Are you ready for bed?
（你要去睡覺了嗎？）

B: Not yet.
（還沒。）

I still need to take a shower.
（我還需要洗個淋浴。）

 實用會話

A: It's been a long day.
（今天真夠忙的。）

I'm going to get ready for bed.
（我要準備去睡覺了。）

B: Me too.
（我也是。）

I need to change into my pj's.
（我需要換睡衣。）

A: While you do that I'll take a shower.
（你在換睡衣的時候，我要去洗個淋浴。）

B: Okay. I'll change and make the bed.
（好的，我去換睡衣，整理床鋪。）

學家片語

bath [bæθ]	名 沐浴；洗澡
relax [rɪ`læks]	放輕鬆
first [fɝst]	首先
tub [tʌb]	浴缸
cream [krim]	名 化妝乳液；雪花膏
forget [fɚ`gɛt]	忘記
uncomfortable [ʌn`kʌmfɚtəb!]	不自在
clothes [kloz]	衣物
pj's [`pi`dʒez]	睡衣（pajamas 的縮寫）
quick [kwɪk]	形 快的；迅速的
change [tʃendʒ]	動 換衣服

15 準備上床睡覺

**要說流利的英語，
準備上床睡覺時也要說英語**

問對方，要睡覺了嗎？

Are you ready for bed?
（你要去睡覺了嗎？）

Are you ready to hit the sack?
（你要去睡覺了嗎？）

Let's hit the hay.
（去睡覺吧！）

我要上床去睡覺了

I'm going to hit the sack.
（我要去睡覺了。）

I'm hitting the sheets.
（我要去睡覺了。）

I'm going to hit the hay.
（我要去睡覺了。）

I'm going to bed.
（我要去睡覺了。）

I'm ready to call it a night.
（該去睡覺了。）

Time to turn in.

（該去睡覺了。）

I'm going to catch some ZZZ's.
（我要去睡覺了。）

不要太晚才睡

Don't stay up too late.
（不要太晚睡。）

道晚安

Good night. Sleep tight.
（晚安，祝你睡得好。）

Sweet dreams.
（祝你有個好夢。）

See you in the morning.
（明天早上見。）

媽媽叫小孩子去睡覺

Time for bed.
（該去睡覺了。）

It's about time for bed.
（該去睡覺了。）

說英語就是這麼簡單

我要去睡覺了

1. A: I'm exhausted.
（我累壞了。）

B: Me too.
（我也是。）

I'm gonna hit the hay.
（我要去睡覺了。）

2. A: Are you ready to turn in?

（你要去睡覺了嗎？）

B: Just about.

（快了。）

Give me ten minutes and I'll be there.

（再十分鐘，我就去睡。）

3. A: Do you want to watch some TV?

（你還要再看一會兒電視嗎？）

B: No. I'm going to bed.

（不，我要去睡了。）

4. A: I'm going to bed.

（我要去睡了。）

I've got to be up early in the morning.

（我明天一早就得起床。）

B: Okay then, good night.
（好，晚安。）

I'll see you in the morning.
（明天早上見。）

實用會話

A: Are you coming to bed?
（你要睡覺了嗎？）

B: Not yet.
（還沒。）

I'm going to do a little reading.
（我還要再看一點書。）

A: All right. Turn the lights off when you're done.
（好吧。你看完之後，把燈關掉。）

B: I will.
（我會的。）

Goodnight, sweet dreams.

（晚安，祝你有個好夢。）

應用會話一

A：Time for bed!

（該去睡覺了。）

B：Do I have to go to bed now?

（我一定要現在去睡覺嗎？）

A：Yes, it's 9:00.

（是的，已經九點了。）

B：But I'm not sleepy.

（但是，我還不睏。）

I want to stay up late tonight.

（我今晚想晚一點睡。）

A：I'm sorry. You've got school tomorrow.

（抱歉，你明天要上學。）

Besides, you need your rest.

（而且，你需要休息。）

B: All right, I'll go to bed.
（好吧，我這就去睡。）

Goodnight Mom! Goodnight Dad!
（媽，晚安，爸爸，晚安。）

應用會話二

A: I'm hitting the sack.
（我要去睡覺了。）

B: Me too. I need a good night's sleep.
（我也是，我需要好好的睡一覺。）

catch [kætʃ]	捕捉
tight [taɪt]	緊的
exhausted [ɪg`zɔstɪd]	筋疲力盡
rest [rɛst]	動 名 休息

MEMO

MEMO

MEMO

國家圖書館出版品預行編目資料

可以馬上學會的超強生活美語 / 張瑪麗, Scott
William 合著. -- 新北市：哈福企業有限公司，
2022.02 面； 公分 . -- (英語系列；77)
ISBN 978-626-95576-2-2 (平裝附光碟片)
1.CST: 英語 2.CST: 文法 3.CST: 會話
805.188   111000809

英語系列：77

書名／可以馬上學會的超強生活美語
作者／張瑪麗‧Scott William 合著
出版單位／哈福企業有限公司
責任編輯／Wendy Chou
封面設計／李秀英
內文排版／八十文創
出版者／哈福企業有限公司
地址／新北市板橋區五權街 16 號 1 樓
電話／ (02) 2808-4587 傳真／ (02) 2808-6545
郵政劃撥／ 31598840 戶名／哈福企業有限公司
出版日期／ 2022 年 2 月
定價／ NT$ 340 元 (附 MP3)
港幣定價／ 113 元 (附 MP3)
封面內文圖 / 取材自 Shutterstock

全球華文國際市場總代理／采舍國際有限公司
地址／新北市中和區中山路 2 段 366 巷 10 號 3 樓
電話／ (02) 8245-8786 傳真／ (02) 8245-8718
網址／ www.silkbook.com 新絲路華文網

香港澳門總經銷／和平圖書有限公司
地址／香港柴灣嘉業街 12 號百樂門大廈 17 樓
電話／ (852) 2804-6687 傳真／ (852) 2804-6409

email ／ welike8686@Gmail.com
網址／ Haa-net.com
facebook ／ Haa-net 哈福網路商城

Original Copyright © 美國 AA Bridgers 公司

電子書格式：PDF